NAKED SPURS

By Karl Smith

orphic house
* UNITED KINGDOM *

Published by  orphic house
* UNITED KINGDOM *

NAKED SPURS:
SCREENPLAY

Published by  orphic house
* UNITED KINGDOM *

First published in Great Britain by
Orphic House
95 Longhirst, Middlesbrough TS8 0TD
Creative Director: Karl Peter Smith

© 2010 Karl Peter Smith
First Edition Paperback 2010

Writers Guild of America, west, Inc.
NAKED SPURS
By KARL PETER SMITH - writer
Registration #: 1236492
Effective Date: 10/29/07

Library of Congress
United States Copyright Office
101 Independence Avenue SE
Washington, DC 20559-6000
Registration Number: PA 1-607-940
Effective date of registration: August 28, 2008
Performing Arts title: Purge the Soul

The British Library
Legal Deposit Office
Boston Spa, Wetherby
West Yorkshire
LS23 7BY
Deposit: August 2010

Orphic House

British Library Cataloguing in Publication Data

Smith, Karl Peter.
 The sound of naked spurs : a spaghetti western screenplay.
 1. Miwok Indians--California--Drama. 2. California State
 Prison at San Quentin--Drama.
 I. Title
 822.9'2-dc22

ISBN-13: 978-0-9566156-2-6

Also available in HARDBACK   *The Sound of Naked Spurs:*
ISBN-13: 978-0-9566156-8-8   *A Spaghetti Western Screenplay*

DOWNLOAD
www.lulu.com

'Encourage the turning of a page.'
- Orphic House

Brief script reading refresher...

<u>Location line:</u>
- o **INT.** (interior) or **EXT.** (exterior)
- o Locations are always listed from **LARGER** to **SMALLER.**
- o **DAY** or **NIGHT** (other times like **DAWN** are unnecessary).
- o **INT/EXT.** A view from inside to outside. eg: Out of a window.

<u>Description:</u>
- o **Describe the environment in the present tense.**
- o **Movement** and **actions** of actors.
- o Possibly a point-of-view **POV** specific to one character.
- o An actor's first appearance is **CAPITALIZED** with a **(micro description).**

<u>Character name:</u>
- o Always CAPITALIZED when followed by dialogue.
- o Multiple names appearing on the same line means **actors talk together.**

<u>Dialogue:</u>
- o **(parenthicals)** guidelines for the unobvious delivery of dialogue.
- o **(...)** three dots **(ellipsis)** OR **(beat)** a **pause** the length of a drum beat.

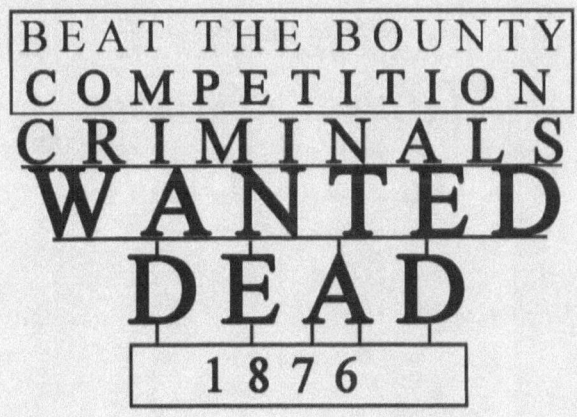

BEAT THE BOUNTY
COMPETITION
CRIMINALS
WANTED
DEAD
1876

CALIFORNIA
MARIN COUNTY

"Marin County, Beat the Bounty,
The wrong caliber need not apply."

- *CHICAGO HERALD, 1876*

SPECIAL ACKNOWLEDGEMENTS

Special thanks to

Toné McGuire
"WYATT EARP"
- Cover design Karl Smith.

And a post'humous CELEBRATION of a life;
the holy man:

Sitting Bull
- Hunkpapa Lakota Sioux
Born: *Grand River, South Dakota*

FADE IN:

INT.   PHILADELPHIA   SUBURBS   BEDROOM   PRESENT DAY

WILD WEST diorama made up of action figures: DAYTONA (dirty bandit) sits on a DONKEY ahead of a line of UNION SOLDIERS.

YOUNG QUENTIN (artist) paints a Coast Miwok Indian warrior.

>   YOUNG QUENTIN (V.O.)
> Every great Western starts with a
> flurry of action. The *Wild West* is
> such a vast topic, too broad to just
> start anywhere. What would my
> History teacher Miss. Prairie say?--

>   MS. PRAIRIE (V.O.)
> --Focus Quentin, focus.

>   YOUNG QUENTIN (V.O.)
> Yeah, she's good at that, focusing--

>   MS. PRAIRIE (V.O.)
> --This presentation needs embellishing
> Quentin. Remember to try your best.

>   YOUNG QUENTIN (V.O.)
> Father also says trying my best is what
> counts and to just *remember* where I
> came from.
>   (narrating)
> One thing my family will *remember* is
> 1876, and today's story, which by
> modern standards surely is considered
> to be an urban legend, of a man, not
> written in any book you'll know of, but
> I will share the story with you all.
> One story told word of mouth to the
> tribes' children around a Lakota camp
> fire. Chief *Sitting Bull* himself spoke
> of a legendary sound; of *Spurs* carrying
> through the mountains which could make
> a newborn baby *smile* and a grown man
> *cry*. This is the legendary tale of the
> man who brought laughter to a nation.
> My great-great granddaddy, *Naked Spurs*.

                         MOTHER (O.S.)
               Quentin! Dinner's on the table,
               it's getting cold!

                         YOUNG QUENTIN
               O.K. ma'am.

Brush CHINKS into a pot of water.

                         MOTHER (O.S.)
               Come and get it I won't tell you
               again!

                         YOUNG QUENTIN
                    (mumbles to himself)
               What a Calamity.

Holds UNION COLONEL in the face of DAYTONA.

                         YOUNG QUENTIN AS UNION COLONEL
               Go get your dinner Kid.

                         YOUNG QUENTIN AS DAYTONA
               Your mouth's sure flapping. Who're
               you sayin' go get your dinner too?
               Who d'ya think you are?

                         YOUNG QUENTIN AS UNION COLONEL
               Your momma.

Moves the DAYTONA figurine closer to UNION COLONEL.

                         YOUNG QUENTIN AS DAYTONA
               Who you bad mouthin'? That mouth of
               yours'll sure land you in a shed
               load o' trouble.

Young-Quentin drops DAYTONA figurine. He notices a fleck of
red paint on his thumb.

                         YOUNG QUENTIN AS DAYTONA
               Colonel you no-good
                    (whispers)
               Son of a bitch -- shot me.

DAYTONA topples over with throaty DEATH THROW noises.

                    YOUNG QUENTIN
            (aloud)
     One second mom!
            (as Daytona)
     I'll get you Colonel.
            (as Union Colonel)
     While you're down there kid kiss
     my...
            (NAYS like an MULE)

                    MOTHER (O.S.)
     You'll be eating the rear of a MULE
     if you don't come get it right-away.

                    YOUNG QUENTIN
            (frantic)
     I'm coming, don't give it to Bengi.

DOOR SLAMS: On the rear hangs an authentic WILD WEST *WANTED*
POSTER franked with the words *BEAT THE BOUNTY — THE GREATEST*
MANHUNT IN HISTORY — CHICAGO HERALD, 1876.

EXT.   SAN MARIN HIGH SCHOOL   DAY

Young-Quentin carries his DIORAMA and waddles towards the
School with a PONY EXPRESS SATCHEL slung over his shoulder.

From car.

                    FATHER (O.S.)
     Can you manage son?

                    YOUNG QUENTIN
     Ok for a lift home tonight dad?

                    FATHER (O.S.)
     Sure. Sock it to 'em kid!

                    YOUNG QUENTIN
     Will do pops!

                    FATHER (O.S.)
     Be sure to give Miss Prairie my
     regards.

INT.   SAN MARIN HIGH SCHOOL   HISTORY CLASS   DAY

WILD WEST memorabilia adorns every wall.

FRONT OF CLASS Quentin adjusts the figures on his WILD WEST diorama.

MISS PRAIRIE sits at the back. She files through a pile of STUDENT ESSAYS which average a few pages each. Quentin's essay is a little light at a mere half a page in length.

CLOSE ON: CLASS REGISTER. A PEN TAPS next to a string of descending letters penciled after Quentin's name; "B-", "C", "C-".

BACK TO SCENE

A seductive tone that every pubescent boy dreams of chirps up from the rear of the class...

              MISS PRAIRIE
      Eyes front. Quentin is telling us the
      tale of his great great grandfather.
      Everybody listen. Please start again
      Quentin. Go ahead.

He gulps.

              YOUNG QUENTIN
      The Wild West.
          (beat)
      The City Marshal's Office; a magnet
      for all criminals.

EXT.   MARIN COUNTY   HIGH STREET   DAY, 1876

LABORERS ERECT A POLITICIAN'S PLATFORM.

Two JUVENILES aim a gun at a tin can.

ELSEWHERE AND WITHIN EARSHOT...

INT.   MARIN COUNTY   CITY MARSHAL'S OFFICE   DAY

(O.S.) GUN SHOTS.

WYATT EARP (MARSHALL STAR) picks his teeth whilst his right
hand DEPUTY paces to the window.

                    DEPUTY
          It' a domestic.

                    QUENTIN (V.O.)
          The prison of Marin County is
          already brimming with criminals.
          Town's getting restless; law-
          abiding citizens are now fighting
          amongst one another.

                    WYATT EARP
          I've already put my feet up. I'm
          off duty.
                    (beat)
          With all the GREAT GUNS idle any
          little puissant can get away with
          murder. This truly marks the end of
          an era. Trains bring in prospectors
          looking for a homestead, all
          shouting God bless America. Once
          upon a time, that would have been a
          hangman's platform out there, now
          it's a politician's. Some suit
          running for Major when he should be
          locking up those kids. Just where
          are their parents?

Onto feet.

                    WYATT EARP
          I'm yet to see a political canon
          that aint all noise. Time's 'a'
          changing; one thing I can guarantee
          is I can still put a stop to this
          juvenile rot. I'm still a force to
          be reckoned with..

Puts on hat. Spurs chink towards the exit.

EXT.   HIGH STREET   PLATFORM   DAY

Wyatt pins a poster *GUN BUYBACK PROGRAM - The devil makes work for Idle Hands, top prices for your pistola.*

SMELLY DOG, an unkempt Mexican pulls up in tarpaulin covered wagon. A rusty barreled pistol hangs from a rotten belt.

>   SMELLY DOG
>   Is that right? You give me good
>   money for my Pistola?

>   WYATT
>   That's right. Even that rusty
>   canon.

Smelly Dog lifts a tarpaulin on his wagon uncovering a cache of some TWENTY-PLUS army issue rifles.

>   SMELLY DOG
>   You like???

LATER THAT EVENING

INT.   SALOON   POKER TABLE   DAY

Around sit four players. HAWK, a fat cigar smoking fur trader pushes a stack of chips into a pile. Smelly-dog puffs upon a cigar. The other two men are non-descript.

>   HAWK
>   That's everything. You either got
>   it or you aint.

Cups the chips and pulls them towards himself.

>   SMELLY-DOG
>   That's a lot of money Mr. Hawk.

Smelly-dog reaches to his belt. Hawk draws his gun.

Smelly-dog carefully lifts the corner of his poncho to reveal a fist sized WAD of crisp cash in his holster. He pulls it like drawing a gun, dumping it onto the table.

                    SMELLY-DOG
            That's everything Mr. Hawk. You
            know I don't count too good, but I
            can sure count on that being a lot
            of cash. Like you say... you either
            got it or you aint.

Hawk rocks back in his chair. His nostrils flare.

ELSEWHERE, IN THE LAND OF THE FREE...

INT.   CHICAGO   PRINTER'S BEDROOM   DAY

PRINTER'S WIFE fastens her bustier around her pushed up half
moons. DOC HOLIDAY (salubrious gent) gives her a hand.

                    PRINTER'S WIFE
            I can hear him coming.

                    DOC
            Your salacious comments tickle me.

                    PRINTER'S WIFE
            Doc, my husband is coming.

INT./EXT.   PRINTER'S   UPPER BALCONY   DAY

Doc throws a medical bag over the balcony into the street.

                    DOC
            I lower myself to the level of
            insects by avoiding greater
            parasites?

EXT.   PRINTER'S   STOREFRONT   DAY

Doc lands and deftly picks up his bag. A HERALD BOY turns
with a "Where'd he come from?" expression.

                    HERALD BOY
            Rag sir?

                    DOC
Pardon?

                    HERALD BOY
Gazette sir? A newspaper?

                    DOC
Why would I want to read about any
one else's exploits?

                    HERALD BOY
Prestige sir.

                    DOC
You'd know about that?

                    HERALD BOY
Everybody loves to read about a
hero sir. Deputies, outlaws. All
good for business.

                    DOC
Quite an educated young chap aint
we?

                    HERALD BOY
Thank you sir. My father owns this
STORE.

                    DOC
Somewhat handy with the news aint
you boy. I bet you know everything
that goes on around here?

                    HERALD BOY
Some would pay to not be in the
papers, if you know what I mean.

Newspaper-boy looks up to the balcony.

Doc swigs from a small bottle of liquor and takes two coins
from his waistcoat breast pocket.

                    DOC
A bright little entrepreneur aint
we?

                    HERALD BOY
          Contains a Stagecoach coupon sir.
          Two for one.

                         DOC
          Who am I going to be taking for a
          ride? Send my regards to your da'dy.

Takes newspaper, steadies his drunken stumble.

                         DOC
                (drunkenly to himself)
          Two for one. I pays for everything
          eventually.

INT.   CHICAGO HERALD   PHOTOGRAPHY ROOM   DAY

WILD FRONTIER backdrop.

CALAMITY JANE, in "DAVY CROCKETT" attire poses with a long
RIFLE; a raccoon tail completes her furry headgear.

The PHOTOGRAPHER crouches with FLASH.

                       PHOTOGRAPHER
               Three -- two -- one. Hold that pose
               Calamity.

BRIGHT SULPHUROUS FLASH

With RIFLE aimed at the top of the backdrop. BANG!

Calamity shakes her headgear free. The backdrop falls,
revealing a romanticized painting of WIGWAMS and TEE-PEES.

                       CALAMITY
               And now... One for the boys.

Swinging her hips out... she sweeps back her hair and her
purdy red lips blow smoke from the long smoldering barrel.

BRIGHT SULPHUROUS FLASH

CLOSE ON CHICAGO HERALD HEADLINE: "WILD FRONTIER" and the flirtatious image of CALAMITY. SUBTITLE: "NO MORE COWS at COW CITY"

BACK TO SCENE

MATCH CUT:

INT.   HISTORY CLASS,   SAN MARIN HIGH SCHOOL   PRESENT DAY

Quentin holds the *CALAMITY JANE* CHICAGO HERALD article and taps his finger on the "NO MORE COWS AT COW CITY" article.

He turns and writes 'Fort Dodge / Cow City' on the board.

> QUENTIN
> Some of you may know, a great
> number of buffalo once roamed the
> plains around FORT DODGE. Prized
> for their hides the town flourished
> from this precious regional
> commodity and COW CITY was born.

Draws a line through FORT.

> COW CITY became a victim of its own
> success; its commodity... the cows,
> slaughtered for their skins were to
> soon vanish from the plains.

Draws line through COW.

> Without COWS, it reverted to its
> former name... DODGE. And so the
> infamous DODGE CITY name was forged.

Circles DODGE CITY.

Quentin picks up the PONY EXPRESS SATCHEL.

MATCH CUT:

INT.   CITY MARSHAL'S OFFICE   DAY, 1876

A MOUNTED MAIL OFFICER holds a PONY EXPRESS SATCHEL.

                    MOUNTED MAIL OFFICER
        Pony express. MAIL!

SOON LATER...

Wyatt, letter in hand...

                    WYATT
        There's only one farming solution
        to infectious cattle; you must
        slaughter the whole herd before it
        spreads like wildfire. The DEATH
        PENALTY for the MURDEROUS inmates
        of Marin County is to be made law
        by decree of Ulysses S. Grant,
        President of the United States
        February 1876.

INT.   MARIN COUNTY PRISON   COMMUNAL CELL   DAY

Wagner's *RIDE OF THE VALKYRIES* scratches to a halt.

CHEWIE, MOUSE and SHADY stand side by side.

DAYTONA waves a thin cane.

                    DAYTONA
        No no no. My granny would laugh at
        you. You're just not intimidating.

Pacing the line...

                    DAYTONA
        Chewie, where's your tobacco?

Chewie opens his maw to show the BLACKNESS inside.

                    DAYTONA
        When I say spit you spit.
            (to Mouse)
        You, *Mouse*. Too quiet! You must
        jangle.

Chewie attaches HORSE BRASS to Mouse's legs.

                    DAYTONA
            Cool, and not too gay.

Daytona pulls Shady's SOMBRERO down to just above his eyes.

                    DAYTONA
            Attitude. Give me more attitude.

Motioning to the OLDMAN holding a needle over a gramophone.

                    DAYTONA
            Take it from the top.

The NEEDLE scratches and the MUSIC continues.

SERIES OF SHOTS A, B, C.

A) Chewie spits a nasty black glob which splats with a
   THWACK onto the floor.

B) Mouse stamps his foot to the sound of JANGLING metal.

C) Shady gives a steely gaze from beneath the brim of his
   SOMBRERO.

                    DAYTONA
            Good, we are looking much tougher.
            Anyone seeing you will definitely know
            you are in my gang now.

EXT.   MARIN COUNTY PRISON   DAY

Prison graffiti reads: *You can book in but you'll never
leave.* A SENTRY trudges across the gateway, rifle slung.

MOUNTED MAIL OFFICER rides in and throws down a mailbag.

INT.   GOVERNOR'S OFFICE   DAY

The GOVERNOR ponders over a letter from WYATT EARP. The

Mounted Mail Officer waits.

                    GOVERNOR
        No one has ever escaped here, let
        alone ever been set free.

                    MAIL OFFICER
        Hey, don't shoot the messenger.

                    GOVERNOR
        Never before have I ever heard such
        cods-wallop.

The Governor lifts a quill from an inkwell.

                    GOVERNOR
        You take this straight back to him.

MUCH LATER...

INT.   CITY MARSHAL'S OFFICE   DAY

Mounted Mail Officer waits: Wyatt reads Governor's letter.

                    WYATT
        Beat the bounty?

                    MOUNTED MAIL OFFICER
        The Governor's idea sir.

                    WYATT
        Instead of executing them, have the
        WIDOWS execute justice.

                    MOUNTED MAIL OFFICER
        Left it up to you to organize sir.
        Can I ask how you intend to carry
        out such a thing?

Wyatt steps up to the window.

                    WYATT
        There may be justice in this world
        after-all. Hey, I'm getting all
        ROMANTIC. Maybe there is one last
        flurry for the great guns. (beat)
        Someone write my words down, this
        day could make me famous.

INT.   PRISON   BACKSTAGE   DAY

Daytona, Chewie, Mouse and Shady stand behind a CURTAIN.
From the other side comes the sound of many men talking.

                    DAYTONA
          Shhh.

Daytona spins the barrel of his pistol and pops it into
Mouse's holster.

                    DAYTONA
          I think you *all* can take them.
          Ready? Give it all you got.

Very serious looks from Chewie, Mouse and Shady. They swish
their poncho's aside and fingers twitch over their pistols.

                    DAYTONA
          Nervous?

Each expresses various degrees of nervousness.

                    DAYTONA
          I think we got 'em where we want
          them. Bring the house down.

O.S. SOUND of clunky communal hall PIANO.

CURTAIN RAISES

SERIES OF SHOTS A), B) and C)

A) Chewie takes a deep breath and spits a nasty black glob
   that splats with a THWACK onto the floor.

B) Mouse steps forward, stamps his foot to the rattle of
   polished metal.

C) Shady raises his head, gives a steely gaze from beneath
   the brim of his sombrero.

Thumbs hooked into belt; Chewie, Mouse and Shady line dance
in front of a crowd of seated Union-soldiers who stamp their
feet and clap along with the piano.

EXT.   CHICAGO   PRINTERS   DAY

A HERALD BOY vends on a street corner.

>   PAPER BOY
>   Beat the Bounty. Read all about it.
>   Beat the Bounty sir. Gazette?

Doc hands over a coin.

>   PAPER BOY
>   Attracting the fastest guns in all
>   AMERICA to the *Wild West*.

>   DOC
>   Not all of them it aint.

CLOSE ON

A banner slung over a politician's platform. *Marin County, Beat the Bounty, the wrong caliber need not apply.*

>   DOC
>   The *Beat the Bounty* needs the right
>   caliber. A competition eh? Well I
>   do like a little challenge.

Pulls "TWO FOR ONE" STAGECOACH COUPON from his pocket.

EXT.   UNION PACIFIC TRAIN STATION   DAY

OLE TICKET VENDOR sits at window. A FLY BUZZES in his ear.
He intermittently swats it.

SIGN 'TWO DOLLARS - MARIN COUNTY RETURN'

NO NAME (tall deft with gun slung) CHINKS across the
platform. His reflection darkens the station window.

The Vendor looks up through the glass. No-name deftly passes
a dollar coin across his knuckles.

                    OLE TICKET VENDOR
          Will you be staying in Marin long?

A match strikes, No-name lights a SNUBBED CIGAR whilst still
passing the coin knuckle to knuckle.

                    NO NAME
          Depends how much of the lame herd
          they want shootin'.

                    OLE TICKET VENDOR
          There's no herd in Marin County
          sir, just passing through eh?

                    NO NAME
          Maybe.

                    OLE TICKET VENDOR
          Two dollars return.

The FLY BUZZES louder in the Vendor's ear.

No-name's coin falls onto the counter -- seemingly spinning
forever with a metallic SHING.

The Vendor gives a belly laugh.

No-name quick-draws. BANG!

Ole-ticket-vendor raises his hands.

                    OLE TICKET VENDOR
          Don't kill me, please.

A crippled FLY twitches on its back near the spinning coin.

                    NO NAME
          I either got it, or I aint.

                    OLE TICKET VENDOR
          One way it is sir?

                    NO NAME
          Is there any other way?

Ole-ticket-vendor shakes head and passes a SINGLE TICKET to
MARIN COUNTY.

Leaning closer to the neat bullet hole in the glass...

                         NO NAME
              Have a nice day.

The Ole-ticket-vendor claws back rickety finger and flicks
the FLY off the counter.

INT.   CHICAGO   SIDEWALK   DAY

Doc stands with a pyramid of suitcases. Calamity juggles a
RIFLE and unravels the 'BEAT THE BOUNTY' poster.

                         DOC
              Don't get me wrong, there's nothing
              wrong with ambition. Although
              you'll find aiming too high in a
              duel will get a lady killed.

                         CALAMITY
              Who said I'm a lady?

A STAGECOACH pulls up. Doc throws suitcases up to the
DRIVER. Calamity boards without Doc ever seeing.

                         DOC
              How much convincing do you need?
              It's a contest attracting the
              fastest guns in the west. I'd liken
              the sport to swatting a swarm of
              insects. No doubt some with
              constitution will just soldier on
              into the night, but it'll be darn
              near a turkey shoot.

Doc looks to the empty sidewalk.

Calamity pokes her head from the carriage window.

                         CALAMITY
              You coming or you just all talk?

EXT.   STAGECOACH (MOVING)   DAY

Rocking back and forth, Doc and Calamity sit either side of a small circular table. Each holds five cards.

Doc wears a black blazer, white shirt and black dickey-bow.

Calamity places a FULL HOUSE, three Jacks and two Queens on the table.

                    DOC
          Bravo. Beginners luck.

Doc's places his cards face down.

                    DOC
          Let me tell you about Dodge City,
          named after the fort, Fort Dodge.
          Nothing like Fort Worth. Ever been
          there?

                    CALAMITY
          Never.

                    DOC
          I'd make it worth your while. I'd
          take you right up the Chisholm
          Trail. I think you'd like that.

                    CALAMITY
          Sounds like I may just swing your
          way.

Doc unbuttons his blazer.

                    DOC
          In my haste it looks like you have
          the upper hand.

EXT.   MARIN COUNTY STAGECOACH (MOVING)   DAY

QUAKERS (HUSBAND and WIFE in classic bonnet).

O.S MEXICAN CRIMINALS HOLLER, bringing the stagecoach to a
halt. PISTOLS of various barrel lengths poke into the
carriage. One invites himself in.

He lifts the lady's petticoat with his gun barrel.

                    MEXICAN CRIMINAL
          Now I don't want you to think that
          we're unreasonable men. You have
          one chance to get out, alive.

EXT.   CHICAGO   STAGECOACH (MOVING)   DAY

Doc in white shirt and no dickey-bow; beneath the table
ankle suspenders hold up his socks; he wears no trousers.

Calamity places a FULL HOUSE, three Jacks and two Queens on
the table.

                    DOC
          Play much Poker? You seem to be
          well versed in the *card art* of
          disrobing a man.

Doc deceives by placing his winning 'FOUR ACES' face down on
the table and unbuttons his shirt.

                    DOC
          Not long before we cross the
          Missouri.

                    CALAMITY
          You mean the Mississippi.

                    DOC
          The Mississippi? Darn. How slow can
          four wheels be?

                    CALAMITY
          I could give you a hand in getting
          you right where you wanna be.

She pulls out a COUPON, TWO-FOR-ONE "UNION PACIFIC".

                    CALAMITY
          A little HERALD BOY pulled some
          strings for me.

EXT.   MOUNTAINS   TRAIN (MOVING)   DAY

A "UNION PACIFIC" STEAM LOCOMOTIVE CHUFFS up a steep climb.

INT.   TRAIN   PENTHOUSE CARRIAGE   DAY

Stumpy RAILROAD TYCOON opens window and flicks cigar.

WIDOW-WHORE sits with all her petticoats flapping.

                    RAILROAD TYCOON
          Too breezy for you baby?

                    WIDOW-WHORE
          No, it's fine.

                    RAILROAD TYCOON
          Cutting the landscape in all
          directions. Centuries in steel.
          Makes you kind-a-proud. You know
          how much steel it takes to lay a
          track from Kansas to Dodge City?

                    WIDOW-WHORE
          Yes.
               (stutters)
          I mean, no.

                    RAILROAD TYCOON
          Twenty-thousand tonnes. Know how
          much labor that takes?

WIDOW-WHORE
Many strong men.

RAILROAD TYCOON
A hell of a lot of strong men.

RAILROAD TYCOON
Have I told you this story?

WIDOW-WHORE
(lies)
No.

RAILROAD TYCOON
Show me an 'engineering feat' said
the President and I showed him
this. Whoever said a man can't move
a mountain?

WIDOW-WHORE
Abraham Lincoln?

RAILROAD TYCOON
It's a metaphor darl', a metaphor
for the resourceful folk that
grafted every rail to the
landscape. Even mountains they
tunnel right through it like a
frigging insect. See this huge
tunnel ahead?

EXT.   TUNNEL   TRAIN (MOVING)   DAY

Approaching the tunnel. Steam powered WHISTLE.

INT.   DINING CARRIAGE   DAY

O.S. WHISTLE.

Widow-whore files her nails. Tycoon rambles...

                    RAILROAD TYCOON
          I'm brokering a lucrative contract
          with the Indians and the Army.
          Young man, a General supplying
          troops to whoever expands the
          frontier. I've heard he's hard to
          barter with. That boy will go far
          if he stays out of trouble.
                    (jogging memory)
          Er...Custer, I'll remember that
          name.

A steam powered WHISTLE SCREAMS in the darkness.

EXT.   MARIN COUNTY   DAY

Wyatt addresses many wagons full of BOUNTY HUNTERS and
homestead WIDOWS.

                    WYATT
          You'll be hunting murderous 'horse
          thieves' and 'embezzlers'; not the
          traits of some of you virgin
          gunslingers. I'm not saying they're
          better shots than I, but I'm sure
          before the day is done, you'll have
          seen the whites of their eyes
          plenty, if you ever live to tell
          this tale. An unarmed man is an easy
          target if you can stomach it. One
          rule and I want you to stick to it.
          Who-ever reaches the Mexican border
          be he armed or unarmed is a FREE
          MAN... hence this competition BEAT
          THE BOUNTY, where a pardon *can* be
          earnt. The rest... Do unto others as
          they have done unto you.

EXT.   PRISON   DAY

Daytona reaches through the bars to a vat of *gruel*.

A PRISON DOLL with a noose around its neck hangs from the
Gruel handle with a letter "NECKTIE PARTY" and a KEY.

Reading letter... Daytona spins the KEY.

>   DAYTONA
>   A cordial invite to a necktie party
>   for all those reckoning on staying.
>   This slop is your last supper and
>   this KEY is for the front door.

A frenzy ensues. Prisoners leap for the KEY.

>   DAYTONA
>   STOP! STOP! You bloody THIEVES! Lets
>   vote for who think they're a leader!

Crowd parts. A powerfully built bald BRUTE steps forth to
oppose DAYTONA.

BRUTE tears up a piece of paper and hands them out.

>   BRUTE
>   This fight will be decided by a
>   democratic vote.

BANG BANG

Brute falls over, two holes around his heart. Daytona stands
holding a smoking DERRINGER.

>   DAYTONA
>   That's settled. The ballot swings
>   in my favor. I'm leader.

He retraces his steps, taking back the slips of paper.

> DAYTONA
> I'll skip my poster campaign.
> I used to lead the best gang in all
> Mexico. They'd take a bullet for
> me. In fact they all took a bullet
> for me. Well actually, from me, but
> that's not my point; my point is
> they never complained, well not
> much. Squealed a little. "Don't
> kill me" in a weird high pitched
> voice which I found quite funny.
> See where this story's going? You
> wanna live, be in my gang. You
> dirty--

Counts the heads.

> DAYTONA
> --Way more than a *dozen*, more a
> *score*. A dirty score? That's not
> catchy. More of a Swarm. The dirty
> swarm? Yeah, the Swarm. And you're
> all my busy bees with a dirty sting
> in the tail.

> DAYTONA
> Any complaints?

SOON LATER...

Daytona masks the length of the two blades of grass in his
hand.

> DAYTONA
> When those gates open it's going to
> be one turkey-shoot. Those who can
> run shall zig-zag and draw fire
> away from me. Those pulling the
> short straw will run first.

He looks around at the bruised scabby legs of most men.

> DAYTONA
> Can anyone run?

A FERRELL BOY, an INDIAN with brighter eyes that the rest catches his eyes.

                    DAYTONA
          Hey you, Ferrell-boy. Do you think
          you can run?

He nods.

                    FERRELL INDIAN
          I can outrun you.

Daytona's DERRINGER presses to his head, then turns it upon everyone else.

                    DAYTONA
          Looks like we got ourselves a
          volunteer.
                    (relaxing)
          Get him whatever he wants.

SERIES OF SHOTS

A dark corner contains a rusty pair of spurs.

A white foam spreads over the FERRELL INDIAN head to foot.

A dirty rag pulls away from the now clean spurs that shine like some new kind of holy relic.

Locks of hair fall to the floor.

Bald as a Coot he flexes his limbs like some naked Olympiad.

THE INFAMOUS BREAK OUT...

EXT.   PRISON   GATE   DAY

VIGILANTES gather outside. Wagons hide a multitude of itchy trigger fingers. QUAKER WIDOWS point many rifles towards the gate.

(OVER) MUSIC ie: 2001 A Space Odyssey

Gate CREAKS inwards.

One WIDOW raises her rifle to the ghostly sound of CHINKING SPURS which fades away.

SILENCE

A TUMBLEWEED passes.

CONTINUE MUSIC *2001 A Space Odyssey*

A lean INDIAN, naked as the day he was born runs as fast as a horse out through the gate, his every step ringing with the sound of chinking spurs…

Open mouthed she looks over her rifle, as do others who wait in ambush.

The bare bottom striding through their ranks towards the horizon mesmerizes the crowd.

MOMENTS LATER

ROAR from the criminal SWARM escaping the prison.

All turn to face the better part of a thousand men surging through the gate.

SPORADIC GUNFIRE and CRIES from FALLING MEN.

EXT.   BLACK HILLS   DAY

INDIANS amongst the towering sandstone buttes...

EAGLE EYES looks down from his vantage point. SITTING BULL (Sioux Chief) sits below with MANY TONGUES at his shoulder. LIGHT FOOT kneels at his side.

                    SITTING BULL
          I am happy you came so soon.

                    LIGHT FOOT
          I am happy brother.

                    SITTING BULL
          Have you heard, the great white
          shark approaches?

                    LIGHT FOOT
          Yes. Do they have horses?

Sitting-bull looks to Many-tongues who shakes his head.

                    LIGHT FOOT
          No horses. We have ample time. Even
          our swiftest could not make Black
          Hills by nightfall.

EAGLE EYES hisses down from his vantage point.

Light-foot picks up his rifle and jogs to join him.

SOON LATER

Many-tongues and Light-foot look down through the buttes.

Sound of CHINKING SPURS

A lean INDIAN hurdles through the rocks near their position.

Light-foot raises his head above the rocks.

                    MANY TONGUES
          Hey you!

The runner slows and looks up.

                    MANY TONGUES
          Yeah you, yes you, naked man with
          spurs.

SOON LATER

All the Sioux huddle, arms folded with stern faces.

Many-tongues faces Sitting Bull, he raises his right hand
covered in colorful war paint.

Sitting Bull nods.

O.S. SOUND of SLAP-SLAP upon bare flesh.

　　　　　　　　　　　　LEAN INDIAN "NAKED SPURS"
　　　　　Ahrh! Wahhrr!

O.S. SOUND of CHINKING SPURS running away.

Sitting Bull, arms folded, stands stern faced.

Naked Spurs CHINKS towards the horizon with a colorful
handprint on each buttock.

Sitting Bull unfolds his arms and slaps his thigh...

...crumples over with belly aching laughter...

...Standing he points in the direction *Naked Spurs* ran and

wipes a tear from his eye then continues to laugh.

EXT.   LOG CABIN   DAY

Daytona and the Swarm watch from the tree-line.

>   DAYTONA
>   It's as good a place as any to hole
>   up. But there aint gonna be enough
>   room for all, better draw straws.

They look at him suspiciously.

>   DAYTONA
>   I promise to not shoot no-one.

Loads his Derringer.

>   DAYTONA
>   (to himself)
>   That's a double-negative if you're
>   wondering. I'm a Mexican.

INT.   LOG CABIN   NIGHT

Around a table stand SEVEN of the Swarm: THOUGHTLESS
BRAWLER, UNSHAVEN TRAMP, TOOTHLESS COOT, OPIUM ADDICT,
BEARDED BUFFOON, FAT CATTLEMAN and Daytona. In a box on the
table lay an apple-pie cut into six pieces.

Daytona looks amongst them.

>   DAYTONA
>   Only six pieces of pie between the
>   seven of us, and I'm guessing
>   every dwarf's hungry? Am I right?

>   THOUGHTLESS BRAWLER
>   What if someone is *really* hungry?

>   TOOTHLESS COOT
>   (lisps)
>   Has a **big** mouth or wants two slices?

Unshaven-tramp looks to the Fat-cattleman.

                    UNSHAVEN TRAMP
            Or has a bigger belly?

                        DAYTONA
            I believe in us all each having a
            slice. But like I said. We're *one*
            too many.

Daytona tips the bullets out of his Derringer 'til only one
remains. He closes the gun and spins the chamber.

                        DAYTONA
            No time to mess about, no funny
            business, I'm just going clockwise.

Cocking the hammer, he aims at everyone in turn, left to
right.

Thoughtless-brawler frowns and steps back from the table.

CLICK

                        DAYTONA
            That would have been way too easy.

Daytona points to Unshaven-tramp's face, his smile drops.

CLICK

Toothless-coot gurns a gummy grin and closes his eyes.

CLICK

Opium-addict opens his jacket showing a tattooed target on
his belly. Daytona points at the bulls-eye.

CLICK

Bearded-buffoon twists the dry ends of his ginger beard.

CLICK

Fat-cattleman breaks from the table and runs for the door.

BANG

Fat-cattleman falls - hand to his back.

Toothless-coot laughs outrageously.

> DAYTONA
> Did you not like him? What's so
> funny?

> TOOTHLESS COOT
> I don't like apple pie.

> DAYTONA
> Well what a predicament, now we
> have a slice too many.

Daytona points the gun at Toothless-coot and pulls the
trigger five times causing him to wince with every CLICK.

> DAYTONA
> Now that's funny. You aint a very
> nice person, but I like you! Anyone
> else not like apple pie?

Thoughtless-Brawler reverses a chair and sits, broad smile.

> THOUGHTLESS BRAWLER
> Isn't APPLE PIE just dandy!?

> DAYTONA
> You wanna die over a stale crust?
> I'm sure who-ever cut it will be
> back soon. On principal, no one
> touches the pie, got it? Now get
> your heads down, we gotta lot of
> running to do in the morning.

NEXT DAY...

EXT.   SHALLOW RIVER   DAY

Thirsty Swarm members rush to drink at the water's edge.

One spots a HORSE grazing on the opposing bank.

> RENEGADE CAVALRY OFFICER
> A horse!?

>   MEXICAN
>   A horse!

The rush escalates into a whitewater stampede.

The Swarm create the biggest white-water fistfight in history. A melee, each trying to be the first to the horse.

Lots of head dunking, garroting and four knuckle sandwiches.

The RENEGADE CAVALRY OFFICER is first over and waves to the Mexicans from the back of his new mount.

>   RENEGADE CAVALRY OFFICER
>   Hasta luego! So long suckers!

He trots away up the embankment.

At the summit he pauses then gallops upstream.

SOON LATER

Mexicans continue to yell at the Renegade-cavalry-officer as they reach the opposing riverbank.

POV RISING OVER THE EMBANKMENT

Reaching the summit they HOLLER with joy and run from view.

Every criminal HOLLERS all the way towards a RANCH full of horses.

30 MINUTES LATER...

EXT. QUIET RANCH   DAY

A broken fence destroys the aesthetics of this homestead.

Daytona swipes dust from his boots.

A DUTIFUL WIFE pulls a small pale of water from a WELL. A large BUCKET nearby lay broken.

>   DAYTONA
>   Hey you! Yeah you.

A HUMBLE HUSBAND and TWINKLE-EYED SON step out of the
shadowy dwelling.

                    DAYTONA
          Fresh water, and a ride.

                    HUMBLE HOMESTEADER
          There *are* no horses left mister.
          I'm lucky they left my plough.

                    DAYTONA
          No bull?

Daytona strikes a match and lights a cigar.

                    DAYTONA
          Still living aint yah, looks like
          you got off lightly.

O.S. WHINNEY from a DONKEY.

CLICK of Derringer at his hip.

INT/EXT.   RICKETY BARN   DAY

At gunpoint the Humble-husband opens the door. His Twinkle-
eyed-son clings to his Dutiful-wife's leg.

CLICK of Daytona's pistol at the Humble-Husband's ear.

                    DAYTONA
          Beggars can't be choosers. He'll
          do.

EXT.   RICKETY BARN   DAY

Daytona secures the barn by padlocking it shut.

Walking the DONKEY to the WELL he offers it a palm of water
and swigs from a half-full PALE himself. A key PLOPS down
onto the water's surface.

                    DAYTONA
          I have plans for us, Donkey. We'll
          go along way together: Mexico.

Chambers bullets, spins it with multiple CLICKS.

The Donkey's ears remain still.

                    DAYTONA
               Hmmm?

BOOM at his ear! The Donkey remains still.

                    DAYTONA
          What's a deaf donkey to me? Could
          be quite an obedient steed. Don't
          worry Donkey I won't have a bad
          word said about you. Guess we
          better be going.

HOURS LATER

EXT.   OPEN PLAIN   DAY

A PEACE LOVING QUAKER and WIFE ride a two-wheeled carriage
along a dirt track. They stop at a Donkey tethered to a
tree. Daytona buttons his fly then raises his gun.

                    DAYTONA
          Go for your gun.

                  PEACE LOVING QUAKER
          Guns - are the weapons of Sinners.

                    DAYTONA
          Do you not think they represent
          free speech? They certainly don't
          separate Saints from Sinners.

Lowers hammer on pistol, taps temple with tip of barrel.

                    DAYTONA
          I'm sure we theologians can think
          of something that can settle this
          theological dichotomy?

SOON LATER

WIFE SCREAMS

Her husband spins, dragged in the dirt behind the carriage.

His tearful Wife runs to his aid when he stops.

>   DAYTONA
>   Back to my point. You were saying
>   I'm a Sinner?

Daytona toys with her husband at the end of his barrel.

>   DAYTONA
>   You may be right, you may walk the
>   *higher* moral ground, but don't it
>   sting like a bitch?

Her husband flinches when she touches him.

He holsters his firearm and she gives Daytona dagger-eyes.

>   DAYTONA
>   Hey, I didn't shoot no-one.
>   (rhetorical)
>   Aint I a Saint.

EXT.   MARIN COUNTY   BLACKSMITH   DAY

BLACKSMITH (muscular bronze) addresses CUSTOMER.

>   CUSTOMER
>   My horse has kicked a shoe.

No-name trots to the post, dismounts and tethers it.

>   NO NAME
>   My horse has *no* shoes; and I have a
>   bigger gun. I'll be back by noon
>   for a fully shoed horse.
>   (tips hat)
>   Gentlemen.

INT.   ZIMMERMANN'S HARDWARE   DAY

MONOCLE (elderly proprietor) with trademark eyewear; hands
Mouse a pair of custom boots. Shady guards the door.

                    MONOCLE
          Ah, the bespoke boots.

He goes out back.

                    SHADY
          Did yaw do what I said?

Monocle returns and shows him the soles.

                    MONOCLE
          'R' for RIGHT and 'L' for LEFT just
          like you said.

                    SHADY
          Saying' my brother's dumb?

                    MONOCLE
          Only one extra dollar. No one will
          ever notice.

                    SHADY
          You chargin' him for being dumb?

Monocle stutters nervously.

                    MONOCLE
          No-no. I just said a dollar extra.
          Call it fifty cents eh? I'm sure
          you boys are returning customers.

                    SHADY
          Put it on the tab.

                    MONOCLE
          No credit sir. I don't keep tabs.

                    SHADY
          You sayin' we're not good for it?

                    MONOCLE
          Now, I d-didn't say that.

                    SHADY
          You sayin' my brother aint got the
          brains to remember twenty-five
          cents?

                    MONOCLE
          I'll open up a tab immediately so
          w-we don't forget the outstanding
          balance of fifty cents.

                    SHADY
          You have a nice day now you hear.
          Just how you think we're to make a
          profit with you all keepin' ripping
          us off?

Monocle nods, gives a compromising wave.

Door chime JINGLES. Enter a HAIRY PROSPECTOR who swaggers to
a pair of scales on the counter. The scales TINK with gold
nuggets.

Monocle brings a tray of weights to the scales.

                    MONOCLE
          That's...

Counter-balances the scales.

                    MONOCLE
          ...forty dollars.

TINK of huge nugget upon the pan.

                    MONOCLE
          Forty-five dollars.

Peels a few bills from a roll of cash.

                    MONOCLE
          Take it or leave it.

The Hairy prospector slams a hand on the dollar bills.

                              HAIRY PROSPECTOR
                    In Chicago Black Hill gold get me
                    ninety!

                              MONOCLE
                    This aint Chicago.

Door chime TINKLES on his way out.

Monocle picks up the weights and goes out-back.

Door chime TINKLES.

SPURS CHINK to the counter.

TINK TINK TINK upon the scales.

Monocle returns with the tray of weights. Places a weight on
the scale and looks up to see three bloody gold teeth in the
pan.

                              MONOCLE
                    Fifteen dollars.

CLICK CLICK of Daytona's pistol hammer drawing back.

                              MONOCLE
                    Not enough?

Daytona's pistol barrel TINKS against the proprietor's
monocle.

                              MONOCLE
                    Twenty dollars?

Again, TINK TINK upon his monocle.

                              MONOCLE
                    Thirty dollars?

                              DAYTONA
                    A fair price to pay wouldn't you
                    say?

Monocle nods.

                    DAYTONA
        I knew you'd see sense. That's what
        they pay in Chicago.

                    MONOCLE
        So I hear.

Daytona folds the money on the counter with one hand.

                    DAYTONA
        If a respectable friend were ever to
        stay in a town such as this, where
        would you say is a fair place?

                    MONOCLE
        The 'Last Chance Inn'.

                    DAYTONA
        You ever stay there?

Monocle nods, then shakes his head. His monocle falls off
into the tray of gold teeth.

                    DAYTONA
        I like you. I think you're a fair
        man, I may be sending some more
        business your way.

Pats his pocket.

Another bloody tooth lands in the pan.

                    DAYTONA
        On the house.
            (double-takes)
        Second thought. Start me a tab.

O.S. GUNSHOTS FROM OUTSIDE

                    DAYTONA
        I hate anyone owing me anything.

Daytona picks up a hat and leaves by the back door.

                    DAYTONA
        Call it even.

EXT.   STREET   NIGHT

DOC zigzags bullets in a drunken stupor; A ROTUND-BANDIT
laughs, another with SHORT-LEGS packs two pistols.

>   DOC
>   I smell something brewing, or do
>   you suffer problem body areas?

Looks Short-legs up and down.

>   DOC
>   Short legs, pregnant, shall I go on?

Short-legs unbuckles both his pistols.

>   DOC
>   I may be way off the trail with my
>   assessment of your candor. You
>   brothers may be just 'style'
>   challenged heathens. I'm not sure.

Rotund-bandit draws a pistol from his shoulder holster.

>   DOC
>   Ah that's a mighty rusty piece you
>   have there fatso, care to slip it
>   back into your Otter's pocket?

Doc unbuttons his waistcoat, it falls down into one hand.

>   DOC
>   I'm unarmed gentlemen, see. Though
>   I am bare-knuckle champion of the
>   'Chicago all boys club' if you
>   fancy a round or three.

Swings waistcoat over shoulder and disarmingly walks away.

>   DOC (O.S.)
>   Look at those stars. Look, the
>   Great Bear. Darn, that one looks
>   like me sucking on both your
>   momma's titties.

Both men run; turning the corner Doc is nowhere to be seen.

EXT.   QUIET RANCH   DUSK

A GINGER FARM GIRL cocks a RIFLE in Calamity's direction.

> GINGER FARM GIRL
> Hands up.

> CALAMITY
> Aint you a little young to be out
> little lady?

> GINGER FARM GIRL
> I'm old enough.

> CALAMITY
> Yeah sure? You look like you're
> about to cry.

> GINGER FARM GIRL
> No I aint.

Calamity draws. BANG!

Legs buckling she hits the floor, blood pours from her knee.

> GINGER FARM GIRL
> (wincing, crying)
> You shot me.

Sobs.

> CALAMITY
> Dumb kid. I knew you were gonna
> cry. Here, I'm sorry.

Calamity covers the wound with a handkerchief.

> CALAMITY
> Next time leave the fighting to the
> big girls. I'm sorry. You'll mend.
> Where's a doctor when you need one?

> GINGER FARM GIRL
> Father's a doctor. He's trapped in
> the barn.

EXT.   CAMPFIRE   NIGHT

Wyatt and a POSSE sleep.

SCREAM from OLDHAND (venerable cowboy)

> OLDHAND
> ARGH! I'm bit.

Wyatt kicks the brush besides his bedding.

There's a RATTLE sound.

> WYATT
> Woh... it's a Rattler all right.

> OLDHAND
> I'm gonna die.

Wyatt trips the crazed Oldhand to the floor. Two red dots
puncture the man's index finger. Wyatt raises a machete.

> OLDHAND
> I'm a craftsman. Not the hand!

> WYATT
> Bite down on this.

A short thick stick now plugs the crazed man's mouth.

Wyatt raises the machete.

> WYATT
> Tuck in any pinkies you wanna keep.

Wyatt CHOPS down firmly.

> OLDHAND
> Mwaaargh!

LATER

Oldhand hand bandaged within a sling sits by a crackling
fire.

                    WYATT
          Just what exactly were you shuffling
          in your blanket that looked just like
          a mouse? You were lucky to have only
          lost your finger.

INT.   HOTEL   BEDROOM   NIGHT

Doc, waistcoat in hand. A naked GAY BANDIT points a pistol.

                    GAY BANDIT
          Take your pants and boots off
          slowly.

                    DOC
          You're smooth. Aint one for
          foreplay are we?

Doc undoes his belt.

                    DOC
          Not even a nightcap?

LATER

Doc sits naked, both hands cover his scrotum. The Gay-bandit
fits Doc's clothes perfectly.

                    DOC
          Now if I knew that was your
          original intention I have a spare
          set in my closet.

Doc opens the closet and shows identical clothes.

INT/EXT.   HOTEL   WINDOW   DAY

Doc sees the Rotund bandit and his Short-legs brother tie up
their horses.

                    DOC
          Oh, just my luck.

INT.   HOTEL   CLOSET   DAY

The Gay-bandit smiles. A pair of PISTOLS with IVORY handles
rest upon a BOWLER. Doc deflates.

>   DOC
>   Not the hat, it's custom-made.
>   Pistols too; everyone knows they're
>   mine, they're unique. Come-awn!?#

MOMENTS LATER

EXT.   STREET   DAY

The Gay-bandit tips Doc's BOWLER hat and crosses the street
away from Calamity and a hobbling Ginger-girl.

>   CALAMITY
>   Doc?

Rotund-bandit and Short-legs exchange looks, they draw and
shoot him... BANG-BANG ...in the back.

>   CALAMITY (O.S.)
>   DOC!

Both men mount their horses and take flight.

Calamity rushes to the corpse.

>   CALAMITY
>   Doc? Doc!
>   (to street)
>   Someone get a doctor!

From over her shoulder...

>   DOC
>   I hear a reputable doctor stays at
>   this abode. Is there a problem?

Without looking at the good Samaritan...

>   CALAMITY
>   I need a doctor urgently.

A HERALD REPORTER (20's) runs to the body.

> DOC (O.S.)
> He's nothing but a darn-robber. I'd
> be more careful in choosing your
> friends missy.

Calamity turns, sees a naked Doc with hands on his scrotum.

> DOC
> Could you please be a lady and pass
> me my hat?

> CALAMITY
> Why you!?

Calamity storms off across the street.

> DOC
> That's gratitude for yah. This
> town's full of nothing more than
> robbers and rude people.

> HERALD REPORTER
> I need a statement.
>   (to Doc)
> You sir.

Doc paces to the hotel lobby with reporter in tow.

> DOC
> Yes, I knew him, quite well. John
> 'Doc' Holliday, a drunkard, a gun
> fighter. A hell of a guy.

> REPORTER
> And you are? Your name sir?

> DOC
> My wife thinks I'm peddling wares
> in Chicago. Keep my name out the
> papers sonny and I'll give you a
> story: Wyatt Earp was once fined a
> dollar for assaulting a prostitute.
> He was onto a good thing 'cause Doc
> said she charged him at least two.

INT.   SALOON   BAR   NIGHT

Daytona downs a *shot* of whiskey. BARTENDER with his fingers
in the SHOT glass lifts it then wipes the counter.

Wyatt rushes in.

                    WYATT
          A ranch has been rustled. A horde
          of criminals calling themselves *The
          Swarm* have made off with all the
          livestock.

                    BARTENDER
          You going after them? It's late.

                    WYATT
          Little chance waiting here for them.

Wyatt gives Daytona a lingering look so he tips his hat and
returns a smile.

Wyatt exits.

                    BARTENDER
          Hey stranger, you ever heard of a
          gang called the *Swarm* led by a
          greasy dago called Daytona?

                    DAYTONA
          Why who's asking?

                    BARTENDER
          Someone came 'round, shouting his
          mouth off. Said he was looking for
          Daytona.

                    DAYTONA
          Are there many people looking for
          this Daytona?

                    BARTENDER
          This one was different; he said he
          was going to kill Daytona.

                    DAYTONA
        This man, did he have a name?

                    BARTENDER
        Lucky criminal? Lucky thief?

                    DAYTONA
        Lucky Crook?

                    BARTENDER
        Yeah that's it. You know him?

                    DAYTONA
        Did he say where he was staying?

He draws a pistol in the Bartender's face.

                    BARTENDER
        Across the street.

                    DAYTONA
        There's a thousand-and-one ways to
        kill a man. This is just six of them.

Downs shot of whiskey.

                    DAYTONA
        If I ever see this Daytona, I'll
        make sure to pass on your message.

EXT.   WILDERNESS TRAIL   DAY

Wyatt prowls the tree-line right of the trail.

Mouse and Shady prowl to the left. Chewie armed with a
double barrel shotgun hasn't seen them yet.

                    SHADY
        Shhh...it's Chewie and he's armed.

Shady raises a pistol and aims for his torso.

Chewie's head appears at the end of his sights.

>   SHADY
>   Chew on this.

BANG

Mouse runs towards the downed shotgun.

>   MOUSE
>   Finders keepers.

Wyatt raises his gun to the rattle of Mouse's HORSE BRASS.

>   SHADY
>   Mouse you dumb mother.

Mouse appears at the end of Wyatt's barrel.

BANG. Mouse falls.

>   WYATT
>   Noisy son of a--

--Twigs snap on Wyatt's flank.

Shady breaks through the undergrowth just as Wyatt raises
Chewie's shotgun.

BOOM.

Shady flies back; the sole of his boot showing an "R".

>   WYATT
>   "R"-sole.

EXT.   DESERT   DAY

UNION SOLDIERS rest. A UNION GENERAL talks to a Herald-
reporter.

>   HERALD REPORTER
>   I'm investigating a death. What
>   unit are you from?

                    UNION GENERAL
        The Army of *The Tennessee*, not to be
        confused with Army of Tennessee or
        The Army of West Tennessee. Which
        became the Army of Mississippi which
        then merged with our Army of The
        Tennessee under Major General
        Ulysses S. Grant?

                    HERALD REPORTER
        So you're in the Army of Tennessee?

                    UNION GENERAL
        No. *The Tennessee* sir.

                    HERALD REPORTER
        The Army of *The Tennessee*?

                    UNION GENERAL
        Yes.

                    HERALD REPORTER
        Not West Tennessee?

                    UNION GENERAL
        That's right.

                    HERALD REPORTER
        Under Ulysses S. Grant?

                    UNION GENERAL
        The very man himself.

The Union-general walks off. The Herald-reporter turns to a
UNION SOLDIER.

                    HERALD REPORTER
        Who died?

                    UNION SOLDIER
        Not sure. Some soldier, if that's
        of any help. From the Mississippi.
        Or the Missouri, wasn't quite
        listening? I hear its good fishing
        up that way.

FLASHBACK: INT.   BLACKSMITH'S   DAY

Daytona lifts a GLOWING HORSESHOE from the fire.

LUCKY CROOK cowers.

                    DAYTONA
          So what'll it be? An eye for an
          eye? Honor among thieves? Huh?

                    LUCKY CROOK
          No!

                    DAYTONA
          Feeling lucky?

Daytona rubs chin. CLICKS fingers and TWO BANDITS hold LUCKY
CROOK by the arms.

                    DAYTONA
          With so many illiterate criminal
          friends, I have to rely on a man's
          word. I'm a fair man. But one thing
          I hate most; is a lazy rustler who
          leaves too many loose ends, fails
          to cross the "I"s and dot the "T"s.

Daytona thrusts a GLOWING HORSESHOE into Lucky-crook's face.

Shrill SCREAM.

INT.   CRIPPLE CREEK BAR   POKER TABLE   DAY

Hundred dollar bills and IOU notes show the importance of
the pot upon the poker table. At the table sit HAWK (a fat
cigar smoking fur trader), DEAD EYES (a blue-eyed cold
killer), WHITE MAN APACHE (a wandering scout of duel
ethnicity) and Lucky-crook (with a hat obscuring his face).

Hawk chews a cigar and fans a winning hand the breadth of
his smile.

                    HAWK
          Full house gentlemen.

Dead-eyes remains motionless. White-man-apache turns over losing cards.

Lucky-crook throws his cards and stands.

>   LUCKY CROOK
>   How could a low-life Vulture like
>   you come to be known as Hawk?

>   HAWK
>   Same reason a <u>loser</u> like you could be
>   called Lucky Crook. Irony I guess.

Hawk tosses him a CHIP.

>   HAWK
>   Here, sit down, we don't want any
>   bad blood between us.
>   (to White-man-apache)
>   No offense.
>   (to Lucky-crook)
>   Come-awn sit down. Rustle up
>   another hand.

>   LUCKY CROOK
>   Screw you.

Lucky-crook pulls his hat down over his face and leaves.

Hawk gathers the cards and receives a stern look from White-man-apache.

>   HAWK
>   Something I said?

Hawk shuffles the deck.

>   HAWK
>   Well are you in or not?

Deals out another hand.

>   HAWK
>   Wigwams don't come cheap.

INT/EXT.   HOTEL   BEDROOM WINDOW   DAY

Daytona tracks Calamity with his pistol, she strides into the centre of the street.

INT.   HOTEL   BEDROOM WINDOW   DAY

FLOORBOARD CREAKS.

Daytona looks to the door. A shadow moves beneath.

>   DAYTONA
>   The Queen's gambit?

Daytona cocks his pistol.

EXT.   HOTEL   DAY

Calamity looks around the street.

INT.   HOTEL   1st FLOOR LANDING   DAY

Lucky-crook holds a double barreled shotgun; he rocks his foot back onto its heel with a SQUEAK.

Daytona's shadow passes under the door of one bedroom.

>   LUCKY CROOK
>   Peek-a-boo.

The twin barrels hover at the keyhole.

BOOM! The door swings inwards with a huge bite taken out.

And he makes a quick CLICK-CLICK reload crossing over the threshold.

INT.   HOTEL   BEDROOM   DAY

SCUFF from within the closet, its door remains open an inch.

Lucky-crook's barrel rises to the dark crack. He eases the
door open with an EERIE CREAK.

Daytona stands behind the main bedroom door, his pistol
points through the bite-sized hole.

BANG BANG

Lucky-crook falls into the wardrobe.

                    DAYTONA
          Guess you're not such a lucky crook
          after-all. Well ya found me.

BANG.

Daytona closes the wardrobe door on a man with a horse-shoe
brand on his face and a bullet hole in his forehead.

EXT.   SALOON   DAY

Doc downs a whiskey, he sees Wyatt's reflection in the bar
mirror. A CUSTOMER stands at Doc's elbow.

                    WYATT
          I once thought I'd lost my morals.
          And you know what? I had. But now
          that I have them back I know right
          from wrong. If we fell out I'd
          shoot your sorry ass in the back.

                    DOC
               (to Wyatt's reflection)
          I'd never forgive you if you do.
               (beat)
          Since when does being an embezzling
          cattle rustler make anyone a
          Marshal? They still blind to your
          many wrong doings?

                    WYATT
          Your mother thinks I'm an
          outstanding citizen.

                    DOC
          You bastard.

                    WYATT
          Draw and I'll drop you quicker than
          you lost your will to be a decent
          human being.

CUSTOMERS at the bar move away from Doc. Doc turns to face
Wyatt. Both attempt to out stare each other.

They laugh like big kids and hug like good old friends,
ending their charade.

                    WYATT
          Doc you son of a bitch.

                    DOC
          No need to get personal. Did I
          mention that I more than kissed
          both your sisters?

                    WYATT
          Brothers?

                    DOC
          Oh dear, that must have been one
          hell of a night, I must have had
          one too many.

                    WYATT
               (to Bartender)
          A bottle of your finest BOURBON for
          this gentleman. Let's celebrate.

EXT.   STREET   DAY

A bunch of *The Swarm* approach, if a tooth aint gold it's
black or missing.

A SCHOOLMA'AM holds a handkerchief to her nose.

                    LADY
          You smelly swine.

                    DAYTONA
          Hey, I hope you're not stereotyping
          me. I'm a nice guy. You'll give me
          a complex.

His henchmen laugh.

                    DAYTONA
               (to men)
          Hey, she hurt my feelings.

Further laughter.

FLASHBACK: EXT.   THEATER   DAY

A PASTE MAN pastes a *ROMEO AND JULIET* poster onto a
billboard. The POSTER depicts a man and woman in Italian
period costume. A HERALD REPORTER sets up his tripod.

CHINK of spurs; it's only Daytona and the SWARM (Chewie and
Mouse, Shady, Toothless-coot and KILLJOY (a tobacco-sucking
ruffian).

The Paste-man's brush shakes.

                    DAYTONA
          We interrupting anything?

                    HERALD REPORTER
          No. It's Shakespeare.

Killjoy stares at him.

                    KILLJOY
          Rome-O and Juli-et?

He spits black tobacco into the Paste-man's bucket.

                    DAYTONA
          No you idiot. Romeo and Juliet.

The Swarm laugh.

                    DAYTONA
          If my pistola be the fruit of love,
          your sister Killjoy would dance on!
          Yeah, I love that dat-opera.

He fires his pistol at the Paste-man's feet causing him to
dance.

The Swarm also fire bullets at the floor and holler. A
bullet strikes the Paste man's foot causing him to fall.

SILENCE

Daytona walks up the line of men, Killjoy's Sombrero tilts
lower than the others.

                    DAYTONA
          You not like what I say about your
          sister? Did I say shoot him?

Daytona knocks Killjoy's sombrero off.

                    DAYTONA
          Can't you see, you just spoilt our
          fun? What a killjoy.

Points up the High Street.

                    DAYTONA
          Run. That way.

Daytona turns his back on Killjoy. Gun in hand he spins his
six barrels and blindly points pistol over his own shoulder.

                    DAYTONA
          Get running.

POV over his shoulder, Killjoy runs up the street.

                    DAYTONA
          Chewie, give me some help here.

Chewie looks over Daytona's shoulder.

                    CHEWIE
        Up, down a bit. Left, left. Hold it.

BANG! A bullet bounces in the dirt at Killjoy's feet.

Daytona turns to see the dirt settle.

                    DAYTONA
        Tut-tut. Come back. Game over! I
        let you live.
                (to Swarm)
        Shall I let him live?

   CHEWIE   MOUSE   SHADY   TOOTHLESS COOT
 (tilts head)   (shakes head)   (nods)   (rocks hand)

Daytona offers his hand to Killjoy.

Killjoy reaches out with a flat HAND like the children's
game 'Paper, Scissors, Stone'.

Daytona's FINGERs are FORKED like a pair of scissors.

BANG

                    DAYTONA
        SCISSORS always **beats PAPER.**

Killjoy falls.

                    DAYTONA
        What? Everybody knows scissors beats
        paper. I'd let him live if he would
        of won. Honest. Cross my heart.

The Swarm remain shocked.

                    DAYTONA
        You no believe me?
                (to Paste-man)
        You believe? Sorry about foot.
                (glances at poster)
        Life's one big tragedy.

Daytona leads the Swarm across the street.

>   DAYTONA
> Chewie, remind me to take *your*
> sister to see Romeo and Juliet.

Chewie gives a stern look.

>   DAYTONA
> What, you think she'll not like it?
> Women love to be serenaded.

INT.   BARBERS   DAY

The BARBER tentatively shaves up to Doc's sideburns.

CLICK of Doc's pistol in his groin.

>   DOC
> That's close enough.

>   BARBER
> I'll not take anything more than I
> aught to.

>   DOC
> I'm just guaranteeing it. Let me
> tell you about my friend Wyatt Earp
> and a little band we created called
> the 'Peace Commission'.

MUCH LATER

INT.   MASSAGE PARLOR   DAY

A MASSEUSE gives Doc a *rosewater* massage.

>   DOC
> Well that's the hogwash I told the
> Barber next door. Still, style
> never goes out of fashion. Neither
> does the smell of an endearing
> rose.

INT.   PHOTOSHOP   DAY

PHOTOGRAPHER and tripod, MISSY (wife-assistant) stands at his side. Doc sits in front of a theatrical backdrop. He holds his chin and leans closer, smiling to Missy.

                    DOC
          Close enough for ya?

The Photographer disappears under a blanket.

A sulphurous FLASH causes stars to twinkle in Doc's eyes.

                    DOC
          Too close?

Doc rubs his eyes then his chin.

Photographer hands plate to his wife and slides another plate into the camera.

                    DOC
          Do try to develop that one, twas a
          real good shave; be a shame not to
          capture it for prosperity.

                    MISSY
          I'll process this plate right away
          Mr. Holliday.

                    PHOTOGRAPHER
          Another?

                    DOC
          Take your time Missy, quality is
          worth waiting for.

Missy gives a demure smile.

                    DOC
          Aint she just flirty? Sure, shoot
          away my good man.

FLASH: More stars in the eyes.

EXT.   STREET   ZIMMERMANN'S HARDWARE STORE   DAY

Doc bites the tip of his cigar.

Calamity smells the air.

> CALAMITY
> (in Doc's accent)
> Do I detect the fragrance of an
> endearing rose?

Doc turns.

Calamity's face lights up.

> DOC
> I do declare myself as a new age
> metro sexual, Calamity.

> CALAMITY
> Nice to see you *alive* and *kicking*.

> DOC
> I don't wish to be rude with my
> hasty departure Missy but a prior
> engagement draws me away from your
> alluring presence. Forgive me for
> excluding myself from your company.

> CALAMITY
> Yeah, see you 'round.

Doc throws her a HOTEL KEY.

> DOC
> Calamity you certainly redefine the
> strength of a woman in both attire
> and aroma. Smell you later baby.

Calamity smells her own armpit.

> CALAMITY
> How rude.

Then looks at the LAST CHANCE SALOON key fob in her hand.

EXT/INT.   LAST CHANCE SALOON   1ˢᵗ FLOOR   DAY

POV through Doc's RIFLE SCOPE through a window across the
street.

He spies the bare flesh of Calamity preparing to bathe.

> DOC (O.S.)
> Oh my, I have surely set a new
> benchmark for deviousness.

In front of a CHEVAL mirror she disrobes, pantaloons first.

> DOC (O.S.)
> Least she's not lost her mother's
> rosy cheeks. What a woman.

A PROWLER with a raised CANDLESTICK reflects in her CHEVAL
mirror. Doc lowers his aim to a shiny waist buckle.

P.O.V. of Prowler through Doc's RIFLE SCOPE.

> DOC
> I declare, a *prowler* in the bedroom
> with a candlestick.

CLICK-CLICK of rifle cocking then BANG!

INT.   1ˢᵗ FLOOR   LAST CHANCE SALOON   DAY

The WINDOW SMASHES.

Calamity SCREAMS.

A candlestick CLUNKS to the floor. Falling to his knees the
Prowler lay bent over with his pants round his ankles.

INT/EXT.   LAST CHANCE SALOON   1ˢᵗ FLOOR   WINDOW   DAY

Across the street she sees Doc tips his hat and withdraw his
rifle through his window.

INT/EXT.   HOTEL   1st FLOOR BEDROOM   DAY

Calamity shuts her curtain.

                    DOC
          Much obliged ma'am. Anytime.

EXT.   STREET   DAY

SHILLING (a cold calculated killer) trails Wyatt up the
street.

Daytona watches the whole from over his own gun sights.

BANG. Wyatt falls.

Daytona watches Shilling open his smoking gun.

CLOSE ON: Shilling's BARREL SPINS SLOWLY, of the five
bullets that fall out each has a name etched on it.

BACK TO SCENE

                    DAYTONA
               (uncocks pistol)
          Hmm.
               (to himself)
          Mr. Shilling, what an intriguing
          game you play.

INT.   DOCTOR'S OFFICE   DAY

Upon the wall hangs a TOMAHAWK AXE and an assortment of
bloodstained ARROWHEADS and BENT BULLETS.

WINCING of Wyatt biting down upon a splint. A sweaty Doc
rummages around his wound with a pair of scissors.

                    DOC
          Darn it.

                              WYATT
                    Easy.

Locates bullet.

                              DOC
                    Here she is.

The bullet TINKS into a pan.

Wyatt pants hard.

Doc grabs a bottle of whiskey and takes a swig himself.

                              WYATT
                    Remind me, never to ask you for a
                    tattoo.

                              DOC
                    Sorry, helps me deal with stress.

Offers the bottle to Wyatt who finishes the bottle.

Doc wipes the bullet on Wyatt's bloodstained shirt and
scrutinizes it closely.

                              DOC
                    Kind of personal.

"WIATT" is inscribed on the bullet.

                              WYATT
                    It's spelt wrong.

                              DOC
                    How fortuitous, a gift from an
                    illiterate well-wisher.

                              WYATT
                    I don't believe in "fate". Man
                    makes his own luck and I am going
                    to spell it out to him, one bullet
                    at a time. Doc hand me my pistol.

Doc gives Wyatt back his pistol.

> DOC
> You're the "Law of the land",
> that's 12 bullets.

Wyatt catches Doc's pistol and slides it into the rear of
his pants.

> DOC
> Got your twelve bullets now.

> WYATT
> You're so literal.

> DOC
> It's what keeps me breathing.

Wyatt exits.

Doc kicks back and relaxes.

> DOC
> Why couldn't I have been a
> gynecologist; Dentist fits way too
> easy on a bullet.
>> (to himself)
> I'm changing my name to Nathaniel
> Zimmerman; or something equally
> long that would not even squeeze
> onto an Indian's tomahawk never
> mind some bullet that's waiting to
> introduce me to my *end of days*.

INT.   TAILOR'S EMPORIUM   DAY

Doc reaches to the Tailor's breast pocket.

> DOC
> May I?

The Tailor hesitates then nods.

Doc takes a tape measure from his pocket and lets it unwind
all the way to the floor.

                              DOC
              Thank you.

Measures the width of his own chest.

                              TAILOR
              Not planning to be with us much
              longer?

                              DOC
              Just the opposite. Any twine?

Tailor points to a ball of string.

INT.   BLACKSMITH   DAY

The Blacksmith looks up; the CLOCK reads 10:45 AM.

Two horseshoes hang from two of four nails.

A glowing horseshoe lifts from the furnace, receives two
BANGS from his hammer then HISSES in a trough of water.

A WET horseshoe now drips from the third nail.

The Blacksmith uses tongs to grasp a small rod of iron.

                              DAYTONA (O.S.)
              Hey Blacksmith.

He turns to see Daytona with a COIN on his thumbnail.

The Blacksmith deftly catches the coin CHINGING through the
air.

                              DAYTONA
              Make me a bullet. And remember to
              make it baby smooth by 12 noon.

MONTAGE

Places COIN into a ladle then the ladle onto some hot coals.

Liquid metal pours into the hole of a two-piece mould.

TAP TAP with a wooden hammer and the mould opens to reveal a bullet with burs.

Blacksmith looks to the CLOCK.

Clamps the bullet in a vice and starts filing it.

INT.   HOTEL   DAY

Shilling opens the curtains to let some light in. Upon the floor lay an open briefcase. A desk holds an array of etching tools. A small vice traps a single bullet already etched with the letters "D" and "A".

He sits and etches a "Y"... with room for further letters.

EXT.   BARBERS   DAY

Daytona enters the Barbers.

He tilts the Barber's mirror to reflect the entrance to the Hotel.

Barber reaches for mirror...

CLICK of Daytona's pistol at Barber's crotch.

                    DAYTONA
          That's close enough.

                    BARBER
          I wont take off more than I aught to.

                    DAYTONA
          That's just how I like it.

INT/EXT.   HOTEL   DAY

Shilling leaves the Hotel and walks towards Barbers.

INT.   BARBERS   DAY

The door bell TINKLES.

Shilling walks right onto the end of Daytona's pistol.

CLICK-CLICK BANG!

EXT.   BARBERS   DAY

Shilling staggers out of the Barbers into the street and
falls beside his own pistol.

Daytona stamps a boot upon the knuckles reaching out.

                    DAYTONA
               (tutts)
          I hear you're quite an engraver?

Shilling winces.

                    DAYTONA
          I'm also known to dabble.

Twists boot causing him to wince more.

                    DAYTONA
          You wanna see? Seeing as though I
          made it especially.

Daytona takes a coin (English Shilling) from his pocket.

                    DAYTONA
          Give you three guesses.

Puts coin in his face and twists boot on his wrist.

                    SHILLING
               (wincing)
          A Shilling?

                    DAYTONA
          Bravo.

Daytona takes out the specially minted bullet.

                    SHILLING
          Made from a shilling?

Daytona's moustache twitches at the corner.

                    DAYTONA
          I like you Mr. Shilling. I like
          your style.

Daytona takes Shilling's pistol, opens it up.

                    DAYTONA
          Let me guess the first name. Hmmm,
          PEDRO? No, that's not me.

Balcony above Daytona CREAKS.

Daytona spins and fires up through the balcony.

PEDRO falls from the balcony.

                    DAYTONA
          Pedro I presume?

The next bullet reads "Daytona".

The bullet bounces off Shillings face then lay in the dirt.

                    DAYTONA
          My lucky day. Who says a man can't
          hold his own fate in his hand?

Loads the shiny bullet made from the English coin.

                    SHILLING
          Confucius?

Daytona lowers the gun to Shilling's head. BANG.

Strikes a match on his boot and lights a cigar...

                    DAYTONA
          That question was rhetorical.

INT.   LAST CHANCE SALOON   NIGHT

O'FLANNEL, an unkempt ginger Irishman with excess nasal hair
looks to the floor where the anemic Doc stares at the
ceiling. O'REIRDEN and O'CONNOR sport healthy beards. All
members of the 'OH' gang wear long trench coats.

Doc regains his feet.

                    DOC
          I am a keen fan of hygiene. And not
          particular to excessive growths;
          nasal hair especially. It blocks
          the respir'...respirator' respi'...
               (sneezes)
          ...blocks the, nose.

Doc smiles.

                    DOC
          Where as, I like to be in the best
          of health, as you can see.

Doc stumbles into O'Reirden and O'Connor.

                    DOC
          Excuse me... aim me towards the bar
          please. Barman, please get myself
          and my new friends here a shot of
          your finest ginger ale. One for me,
          and one for these ginger men... I
          mean gentlemen.

MOMENTS LATER

O'Flannel, O'Reirden and O'Connor run into the street
searching for something.

                    O'FLANNEL
          Just where'd he go? No one's that
          fast.

SOON LATER...

INT/EXT.   PHOTOSHOP   NIGHT

CREAK of floorboard outside on the veranda.

O'Flannel's silhouette appears at the window.

Then a gun barrel pokes in round the opening door.

A sulphurous FLASH in his face of O'Flannel blinds him.

                    O'FLANNEL
          WAHHH!

                    DOC
          God that nostril hair's gotta be
          all short 'n' peachy.

Doc runs and hides.

MOMENTS LATER

INT.   PHOTOSHOP   NIGHT

The door creaks open.

Doc looks through a *flap* in the canvas backdrop, through a
HANDSOME KNIGHT's VISOR in a depiction of SLEEPING BEAUTY.

Enter O'Connor, O'Flannel and O'Reirden.

                    O'CONNOR
          Call it da luck o' da Irish, but
          it's like those eyes are just
          following me 'round da room.

                    O'REIRDEN
          Your knight in shining armor.

Doc sees O'Flannel's burnt face down the end of a barrel.

                    DOC
          Is this where I say cheese?

They all open fire. BANG BANG BANG Doc stumbles back onto
his butt. A tight grouping of bullets puncture the depiction
of the Knight's breastplate.

                              O'FLANNEL
              And dee all lived happily ever
              after.

Laughter over smoking guns.

As the smoke clears...

Missy appears in a nightgown. Doc is beneath the canvas.

MOMENTS LATER

The Photographer and Missy unravel Doc.

Opening his perforated shirt reveals a dented *photo plate*
held with heavy-duty string. The plate is a 'close up'
NEGATIVE of Doc holding his chin.

Opening his eyes he rubs his chin.

                              DOC
              I told you it was a close shave.
                    (beat)
              This has gotta hurt in the morning.

EXT.   FORT EDGE OF FRONTIER   4 DAYS LATER

Daytona rocks back and forth on his donkey for miles.

He rides right up to the POSTMAN sat outside and throws down
a MAILBAG.

                              DAYTONA
              Pony Express! I hope there's no
              perishables.

POSTMAN appears.

                              POSTMAN
              The Pony Express doesn't come this
              way.

                              DAYTONA
              It does now.

JACOBS, a uniformed soldier walks by.

> DAYTONA
> Hey, soldier, where you stationed?

> JACOBS
> Fort Atkinson. I'm Lieutenant Jacobs.

> DAYTONA
> Fort Atkinson? I think I got a
> letter from your momma.

Jacobs picks up the mailbag. Daytona pats him on the back.

> DAYTONA
> Sorry to hear about your dog. No
> news is good news as they say.

> JACOBS
> You read my mail?

> DAYTONA
> It was a long journey, I got bored.
> And I can't read too good. Now you
> got us *both* crying.

Jacobs riffles through the torn letters.

A sign reads "MEXICO THAT WAY".

Daytona looks to Jacobs then the sign.

> DAYTONA
> Need I ask how far?

EXT.   DESERT   MEXICAN BORDER   DAY

The wind whips up a tumbleweed.

Daytona crouches over his lame Donkey.

A TWIG snaps underfoot. No-name stands with short toothpick.

Daytona spins round, his hand hovers over an empty holster.

                    DAYTONA
        Huh?

No-name holds Daytona's gun.

                    NO NAME
        Now what would a lame donkey be
        doing out here with a loser like
        you???

                    DAYTONA
        You looking for someone mister? You
        going to shoot me with my own gun?

                    NO NAME
        Tut-tut. In your delirium you've
        overlooked that your pony there
        seems to be in quite some pain.

Tumbleweed rolls by.

                    NO NAME
        The nations who know this pass well
        say a *stink* blows towards Mexico.
        Anything that gets up my nose seems
        to also run that way.

                    DAYTONA
        What is it you want?

No-name opens Daytona's pistol.

                    NO NAME
        You don't happen to know anyone
        around here that's ran all the way
        from Marin County now do ya?

                    NO NAME
        Five in the barrel?

No-name lets bullets drop to the floor.

                    NO NAME
        Eenie, Meanie, Minie and now *Moe.*

The gun THUDS in the dirt at Daytona's feet.

> NO NAME
> Now we both know that leaves you
> only one bullet.
> > (beat)
>
> But you got options. The way I
> figure this is; in a sick but
> satisfying game of Russian
> roulette, you can put your sick
> donkey out of its misery and then
> hop on over to Mexico hoping I just
> don't shoot you; or likewise risk
> having a shot at *me* with the
> knowledge that-that lame donkey
> will out live *your* sorry ass.

No-name CLICKS back the hammer on his pistol.

Daytona without breaking eye contact picks up the gun and
slowly turns the barrel towards the Donkey's head.

CLICK-CLICK... CLUNK of an empty chamber.

No-name breathes in.

CLICK-CLICK... CLUNK.

Daytona squints.

Again... CLICK-CLICK... CLUNK.

> NO NAME
> It's getting kind-a tense aint it?

CLICK-CLICK... CLUNK

Daytona's eyes flit side to side.

CLICK-CLICK

Daytona and No-name stare intently at each other.

> DAYTONA
> You know what separates Saints from
> Sinners?

> NO NAME
> You plannin' takin' the answer to
> your grave?

Points to Mexican border with toothpick.

> NO NAME
> If that aint the route you plan on
> taking, who's gonna be tellin' your
> story?

Daytona sighs. BANG! The Donkey is put out of its misery.

LONG PAUSE

> DAYTONA
> You love animals or somethin'?

> NO NAME
> Somethin'.

Daytona turns slowly. Walks slowly towards Mexico.

> NO NAME
> You *know* reaching the Mexican
> border makes a free *man*?

> DAYTONA
> You don't say.

> NO NAME
> No, I said it. Take my advice,
> watch those double-negatives, one
> may get the wrong impression and
> not take too kindly to it.

> DAYTONA
> You a Saint?

> NO NAME
> No, I'm still planning on shooting.
> Just thinking how inconvenient
> dragging your corpse back would be.

MONTHS LATER

INT.   HIGH COURT 'STATE VS. WYATT EARP'   DAY

CITIZENS bustle into a packed out hall. JUDGE conducts all
proceeding from his podium with an OFFICER at his side. The
PROSECUTION resides left of center. Prosecution stands.

                    PROSECUTION
          Your Honor. The State versus, Mr.
          Wyatt Earp.

                    JUDGE
          The defendant?

                    OFFICER
          Call the defendant.

WYATT EARP (bearded) enters and walks the long mile to the
dock; puts his hand on the Bible in the Officer's hand.

                    OFFICER
          Repeat after me. Do you swear by
          almighty god to tell the truth, the
          whole truth and nothing but the
          truth so help you god?

                    WYATT
          Too fucking right I do.

Citizens gasp.

                    JUDGE
          Quiet please.

Judge BANGS gavel, nods to the Officer.

                    OFFICER
          Please confirm your name.

                    WYATT
          Wyatt Earp.

CHIT CHATTER from court.

BANG BANG, gun like gavel from Judge.

                    JUDGE
     I call for *order!* *Order!*

Judge motions to the paper shuffling PROSECUTION who brings
a copy to the bench and hands it to the Judge.

                    PROSECUTION
          Mr. Earp?

Wyatt stares.

                    PROSECUTION
          February fifteenth, in the year of
          our lord 1876, mean anything to you?

                    WYATT
          Not particularly.

                    PROSECUTION
          How about Marin County?

                    WYATT
          I heard of it.

                    PROSECUTION
          A criminal outpouring... Inmates of
          Marin County; some one-thousand-
          men, broke out... and in what can
          only be described as an act of
          genocide; were systematically
          hunted down and slaughtered like
          cattle. How do you plea?

                    WYATT
          Guilty.

All gasp.

The judge leans forward.

                    WYATT
          Though, I can't take all the credit
          for it. I did have some help.

LATER IN THE PROCEEDINGS...

Doc and Calamity sit in the public gallery.

> PROSECUTION
> Is it *not* fair to say that this
> leader of the *Swarm*; this Daytona
> as you have named him; had what's
> commonly called a face-off, with a
> man with no name? And he was
> killed? Is it not so farfetched to
> assume that if one thousand men
> died by your hands. That he was
> shot too?

> WYATT
> I'd say that was a fair assumption,
> but it's not the truth.

> JUDGE
> Stop leading the jury.

> PROSECUTION
> Many men and women, led by the *then*
> acting Marshal, Mr. Earp here, seem
> to have been a law unto themselves.
> As an intelligent Jury, do you
> believe this man's tale? Or do <u>you</u>
> of sound mind think that this woven
> cacophony; this intricate story
> recorded by his own biographer,
> Stuart Lake be nothing more than
> the tallest of *said* Indian folklore
> fairytales?

> JUDGE
> Will the jury retire to make its'
> verdict?

> WYATT
> Can I speak your Honor?

Judge nods.

Wyatt stands and waits till all settle and are listening.

WYATT

The job of Marshalling this land has
always been turned town by the tamest
of men, and woman for that matter.
And I of all people know that justice
which ends in the death of one man
let alone many - must have a trial
and many of these trials are fraught
with uncertainty.
>   (beat)
These citizens are baying for my
blood. Let me tell you *Your Honor*,
life is no cheaper in the *west* than
in the *east*; though the availability
of guns has made the shedding of
one's blood a little easier.
>   (beat)
In my defense I want you to know
that this land is a calmer place
for what I and some others in this
room were ordered to set in motion.
Those who can *now* walk the *quiet*
parks and play with their children
in the *quiet* streets must remember
one thing. In such a short time you
forget that life was a lot wilder
in the *west*. And yes, I was law
unto myself, there was no one else.
>   (beat)
I don't know how easy your lives
have become but it's a darn lot
easier than any who still have to
look over their shoulder 'cause
they walk in moccasins.
>   (beat)
It's one mass slaughter. There are
no more cows in cow city. No more
food for the land of moccasined
feet. This is slowly becoming no
country for old men, so *you* think
long and hard whether you want this
neck-tie party to go ahead, or
whether you'd give a man a chance
and let a man run for his life like
we did back in February 1876.

> JUDGE
> I would like to adjourn the
> proceedings till first thing
> tomorrow. I'm sure the Jury would
> like time to consider its final
> verdict?

JURY FOREMAN nods.

EXT.   HIGH COURT 'STATE VS. WYATT EARP'   DAY

Laborers erect a hangman's platform.

A smoke ring appears from beneath an onlooker's Sombrero.

> ONLOOKER IS DAYTONA (V.O.)
> Saints and Sinners? Now if I was to
> take the moral high ground, to go
> in there and tell the truth; he'd
> be a free man and I'd be the one
> with the noose round my neck.
> (beat)
> Who am I to take the moral high
> ground? Puts a man between a rock
> and a hard place.

Deep puff.

Throws down cigarette and twists boot over it.

He glances at the gallows noose and walks away.

Continues walking.

> DAYTONA (V.O.)
> Must be a hard call, judging the
> fine line between a *Saint and a
> Sinner*. The thought of an innocent
> man swinging sickens even *me* in the
> pit of my stomach. A last man's
> thought would be that nipping rope
> at his throat. Whether he's right
> or wrong I bet it stings like a
> bitch.

INT.   HIGH COURT 'STATE VS. WYATT EARP'   DAY

Wyatt cuts a fat cigar into shape and the attending Officer
lights it.

> WYATT
> Much obliged. Thank you Your Honor.
> (beat)
> I never liked your *General Custer*; and
> after he promoted the mining of the *gold*
> Hills, *Sitting Bull* didn't like him
> either; it's his peoples' land, I saw
> the man's point, didn't take much to
> empathize, but that wasn't enough to
> justify any wanting the man dead.
> (beat)
> I along with the help of *others* waited
> in the hills with Sitting Bull; waiting
> for *The Swarm*.
> (beat)
> Then, Chaos... a *hell on Earth* is the
> only way to describe what happened next.
> We watched the two parties converge from
> our relatively safe vantage point.
> Custer's men and *The Swarm* were below
> cutting chunks out of each other. Yes
> there was a battle.
> (beat)
> As for the disgraced survivor...

EXT.   EN ROUTE TO THE MEXICAN BORDER   DAY

A mule trots along...

It's rider *General Custer*, wears a Sombrero.

The mule buckles underfoot.

MOMENTS LATER... CLICK-CLICK OF A PISTOL COCKING

> NO NAME
> Now we both know you got two
> options.

FLASH FORWARD TO THE PRESENT DAY

INT.   SAN MARIN HIGH SCHOOL   HISTORY CLASS   DAY

Young-Quentin stands behind his WILD WEST diorama. Miss
Prairie gives a sign to wrap up his presentation.

> YOUNG QUENTIN
> (SIGHS)
> And so the sun set for the last
> time for Mr. Earp. The town in
> which he was *tried* became nothing
> more than a ghost town. Many Bounty
> Hunter's that came from afar were
> buried in them hills. Wyatt was
> never again to look from that City
> Marshal's Office.
> (beat)
> His memoirs, told to biographer
> Stuart Lake recorded only a sense
> of what truly happened and a few
> posters remain.

School BELL RINGS. A few chairs screech.

> MISS PRAIRIE
> One moment!

Miss Prairie taps her pen upon her clipboard. The whole
class claps and cheers.

> MISS PRAIRIE
> Quentin, you certainly know how to
> tell the tallest of tales; and a
> wild one at that.

Screech of chairs.

> MISS PRAIRIE
> A paragraph on the *WILD WEST*'s law
> makers or breakers! Usual number of
> words by Monday.

Pupils groan.

MINUTES LATER EVERY PUPIL HAS GONE

Miss Prairie collects the text books from each desk.

Beneath the Wild West DIORAMA lay Quentin's old PONY EXPRESS mailbag.

Moments later, in her hands... A sepia photograph and on the table a pair of Wild West SPURS.

>   MISS PRAIRIE
>   Oh my. Surely not.

She flicks her eyebrows upwards.

MOMENTS LATER...

INT.   STAFFROOM   SAN MARIN HIGH SCHOOL   DAY

Miss Prairie leans against the PHOTOCOPIER apple in hand.

The copier flashes and chugs into motion.

She lifts a COPY from the TRAY and laughs hysterically; and bites hard into the apple.

CLOSE ON: Chicago Herald article: A man's ass with a colorful SIOUX handprint on each buttock. Across his chest he wears a banner. "I BEAT THE BOUNTY".

>   MISS PRAIRIE
>   *Naked Spurs?*

She chuckles. In the OUT TRAY lands copy upon copy of the bare man's BUTTOCKS.

An old letter in her hand reads:

>   MISS PRAIRIE
>   To the man I call a friend.

She unfolds the letter inside.

FLASHBACK TO 1876

EXT.   BLACK HILLS   SUNSET

A campfire flickers amongst the towering sandstone buttes.

INDIAN CHILDREN sit listening to Chief-Sitting-Bull.

> SITTING BULL   MISS PRAIRIE (V.O.)
> (in Cheyenne accent)   (storytelling)
> In this very place,   In this very place,
> the distant sound of...   the distant sound of...

> SITTING BULL
> ...spurs traveled like a wind
> through the hills.
>   (beat)
> Then he appeared, the man who could
> run swift like horse.

Chief-Sitting-Bull points to the horizon.

> SITTING BULL
> The man with no gun, looking not
> for a fight, but for freedom.

MATCH CUT TO:

AUTHOR'S FOOTNOTE:
    Flick through THUMBNAIL images (top right) to see the
    envisioned MATCH CUT transition.

EXT.   SITTING BULL MONUMENT   SUNSET, PRESENT DAY

Reveal the sun at the fingertip of the gargantuan rock
carving that is Sitting Bull.

The carved face of Sitting Bull stares down an outstretched
arm upon which stand Miss Prairie with a group of students
from San Marin High School.

              SITTING BULL (V.O.)   MISS PRAIRIE
               (Cheyenne accent)   (reading)
             You too may one day   You too may one day
             bring your children...   bring your children...

                         MISS PRAIRIE
              ...to this very spot and one day tell
              them of the same swift-footed man, the
              legend of laughter we have named as
              Naked Spurs.

POV RISING LIKE A BIRD INTO THE SKY.

                         MISS PRAIRIE
              You are welcome here anytime; your
              appearance will bring many years of
              great merriment to our children and
              our children's children. You will not
              be forgotten.
                         (beat)
              Your good friend, Sitting Bull.

THE GHOSTLY SOUND OF SPURS PEAKS AND THEN FADES.

THE LOVELY LAUGHTER OF SITTING BULL ECHOES.

                                              FADE OUT:

                         THE END

"The story of a sound, sounds like a great story."

**"If you completely storyboard a movie you neuter possibilities for happy accidents"
- Gore Verbinski, *Director of Pirates of the Caribbean: Curse of the Black Pearl.***

A story that will appeal to general readers and classicists alike.

When the reputations of two gods hinge on the actions of one man expect all hell to break loose when gun-toting Argonauts descend all-guns-blazing to the Underworld.

Orpheus's wife is not quite dead yet!

He must find her.

"Clutching my sister, heavy, dead in my arms; my cries for help drowned out by the music of the Pool hall. One Greek hero had been here before me; Orpheus."
- Karl Peter Smith, *The Author.*

email: orphichouse@yahoo.co.uk   titles available from all good book stores

Greek mythology

Comic book, strips

Graphic Novels

FICTION

SEARCH FOR EURYDICE:
SCREENPLAY AND GRAPHIC NOVEL

HARDBACK
ISBN 978-0-9566156-6-4

PAPERBACK
ISBN 978-0-9566156-0-2

BOOK SIZE: US LETTER 8"x11.5"

KARL SMITH

Serial Pool Attendant

SCREENPLAY

WRITTEN BY KARL SMITH

Alexandra Vino   *Brian Spangler*

TV PILOT & SERIES BIBLE

Keeping **L.A.** clean is just MURDER.

* Includes the 24 PAGE 'Bible' for the TV Series. *L.A. Serial Pool*
A minute by minute breakdown of the 'Hero's Journey' for TV.
(p.84-107.)
Four-Act Structure, where Act breaks match commercial breaks.
An insight into ABC, CBS, NBC, FOX, and new BBC TV format.

SERIAL POOL ATTENDANT

Synopsis:
On an L.A. beach Alex (pool attendant) meets her idol, the notorious Shark (real name Henry, a high profile killer on parole). Shark mentors Alex in the art of 'murder' and in 'not getting caught'. Cultural references lead to his catchphrase . . .

"A CLASSIC!"

The big reveal: Shark is not just a serial killer but a puppet taking orders from Victoria (once screenplay tutor to Alex) and mission director of an assassin-like organisation known as the . . .

'SERIAL POOL'

It is not mere chance that brings Alex and Henry together.

Siblings with a flair for death. Shark takes his sister under his wing.

Hitmen liaising as *real CLEANERS.*

"IF YOUR PROBLEM IS TOO BIG TO FILTER . . .YOU CALL THE POOL ATTENDANT"

Concept:
Two loyal Psycho's team up to create the L.A. version of "Miami Vice". Add a sexy mission director... Victoria... a sprinkling of "Mission Impossible" and that's ENTERTAINMENT!

"YOU'LL DIE LAUGHING"
"...lunatic brother-sister psychology at its finest."

About the Author
Karl Smith graduated with a degree in Fine Art from Cleveland College of Art and Design. His fresh fusion of action and emotion when screenwriting is surely to be seen in a cinema near you soon. Bet your mortgage on it!

A HISTORY OF FEAR

SCREENPLAY

SCREENPLAY
WRITTEN BY
karl smith

"Will put the frighteners up you."
"A GRIPPING TALE!"

A HISTORY OF FEAR

Synopsis:
A wish melds the soul of a kind-hearted simpleton to a toy BEAR. A secret for three generations, the seven foot GUARDIAN wakes in time of need.

Surviving the sinking of the TITANIC a toy BEAR passes into the hands of the JEWISH COMMUNITY. Aboard the rescue ship CARPATHIA it travels on to the gas chambers of AUSCHWITZ.

The BEAR brings something with it...A HISTORY OF FEAR.

When TRICK OR TREATERS uncover an SS OFFICER in the neighborhood . . .

HALLOWEEN IS ABOUT TO GET A LITTLE HAIRY

Concept:
'Gremlins' meets 'Schindler's List' / 'The Golem of Prague'.

email: orphichouse@yahoo.co.uk   titles available from all good book stores

Teddy bears
Juvenile drama
Jewish faith

ORPHIC HOUSE

A HISTORY OF FEAR:
SCREENPLAY

HARDBACK
ISBN 978-0-9566156-9-5

PAPERBACK
ISBN 978-0-9566156-3-3

KARL SMITH

naked spurs

'Moving words around a page is like painting.'
To learn this process check out... Print-on-demand Technical Guide: Screenplay Publishing

Karl Peter Smith

Pencil Drawing of Miss. Helen Shepley by K.S. 2006.

E-PORTFOLIO:
1. Search for Eurydice - Romance with Bite
2. Serial Pool Attendant - Crime
3. Naked Spurs - Western
4. A History of Fear - Horror
5. Purge the Soul – Thriller
6. Memoirs of Dirty Max - Romance
7. Bikini THREE-20 (Thunderbirds) – Sci-Fi
8. Bill and Ted's Idiot's Guide to Screenwriting - Comedy

EDUCATION
UNIVERSITY OF TEESSIDE, Cleveland, England.
Bachelor of Fine Art - Printing, Drawing and Painting.
Specialized in Sculpture

HONOURS
Cleveland College of Art and Design used my sculptures to advertise the college in the UCAS prospectus; a national publication attracting future students to campus.

"I cried whilst writing."
A History Of Fear
"...the blonde ponytail."

Thanks Helen x

DAYTONA (Johnny Depp)

LYRICAL BARD (Vanessa Paradis)

Author's note:

Even though I do not know the words
the beauty of the song and the singer,
and the moment it evokes
is multi-cultural.

Listen, and be seduced.

Alizée's - Mes courants électriques / Gourmandises

Picture *Vanessa Paradis* rising in a Hot Air Baloon.
Singing as the credits rise...

The End.

www.ingramcontent.com/pod-product-compliance
Lightning Source LLC
Chambersburg PA
CBHW030149200626
46812CB00016B/1764